**by Alison Reynolds**

illustrated by Alan Brown

*Engage Literacy* is published in the UK by Raintree.
Raintree is an imprint of Capstone Global Library Limited, a company incorporated in England and Wales having its registered office at 264 Banbury Road, Oxford, OX2 7DY – Registered company number: 6695582

www.raintree.co.uk



10 9 8 7 6 5 4 3
Printed and bound in India.

Max Jupiter

ISBN: 978-1-4747-1790-8

# Contents

## Chapter 1

# Hold on!

Max Jupiter Astro Marriot looked through the porthole at Earth. The planet Earth looked like a blue ball from space.

Every holiday Max visited outer space with his astronaut parents. They belonged to a secret group called Space Guards, which protected Earth from danger.

Max stretched. It was peaceful floating in orbit 300 kilometres above Earth.

Suddenly, the spaceship bucked up and down like a horse. "What's happening?" said Max. He was clinging onto a railing.

"Hold on!" shouted Dad. "Meteor shower."

Max's parents leaned over the screen.

"Can I do anything?" Max ran across the space deck.

"Buckle up!" said Dad. "We'll figure it out."

Max slid into his seat. His parents always thought he was too young to help. Max wanted to be a Space Guard more than anything else in the universe.

"Change course!" Mum shouted, staring at the screen. "Hundreds of them are coming towards us."

Dad's fingers raced over the switches. The spaceship turned left.

Mum grinned. "All safe now," she said.

"I'll check for damage," said Max. He then turned on the computer screen in front of him.

"Those meteor showers weren't predicted," Mum said to Dad.

Max gasped. "Oh, Mum!"

"Wait, Max, I'm busy."

"Mum, Dad. You might want to..."

"In a minute, Max," said Dad.

"Look!" shouted Max.

A huge asteroid filled the screen. It was heading directly towards Earth.

## Chapter 2

# Big trouble!

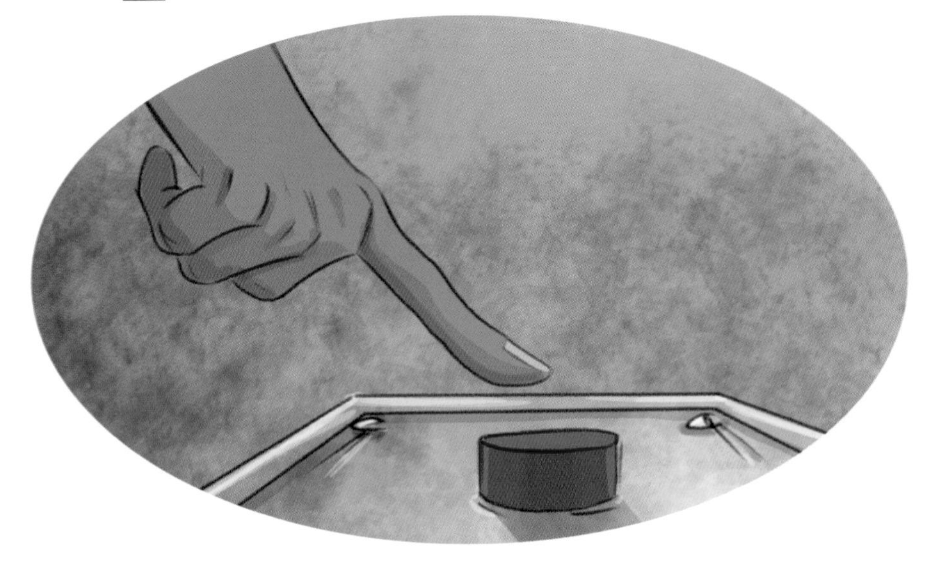

"It's as big as a small planet," said Max.

"It's trouble," said Mum. She pressed the emergency button.

Then, she and Dad began sending asteroid data back to Earth. The data told how big it was and where it was headed.

Max wondered how they could be so calm. This was *Scary* with a capital S! This could be the end of life on planet Earth!

That was how dinosaurs died out 65 million years ago. That's what some scientists said. An asteroid had hit Earth in the country of Mexico. It made a huge dust cloud that caused massive climate change. Max shuddered.

That asteroid had only been 16 kilometres across. This one was hundreds of kilometres across.

Max started to snap photos of the asteroid on his screen. He spotted something strange – booster rockets. What were they doing there?

Those sudden meteors were strange. Meteor showers were often caused by rocks breaking off an asteroid after a crash.

"The speed is 45,200 kilometres per hour," said Dad. His face was whiter than the Moon.

"How long until impact?" asked Mum.

"One hour and fifteen minutes," said Dad.

Suddenly, the radio buzzed to life, "Rescue Space Guards to Space Guard 1. Request permission to dock."

Mum blurted out, "Permission granted. This is a big emergency."

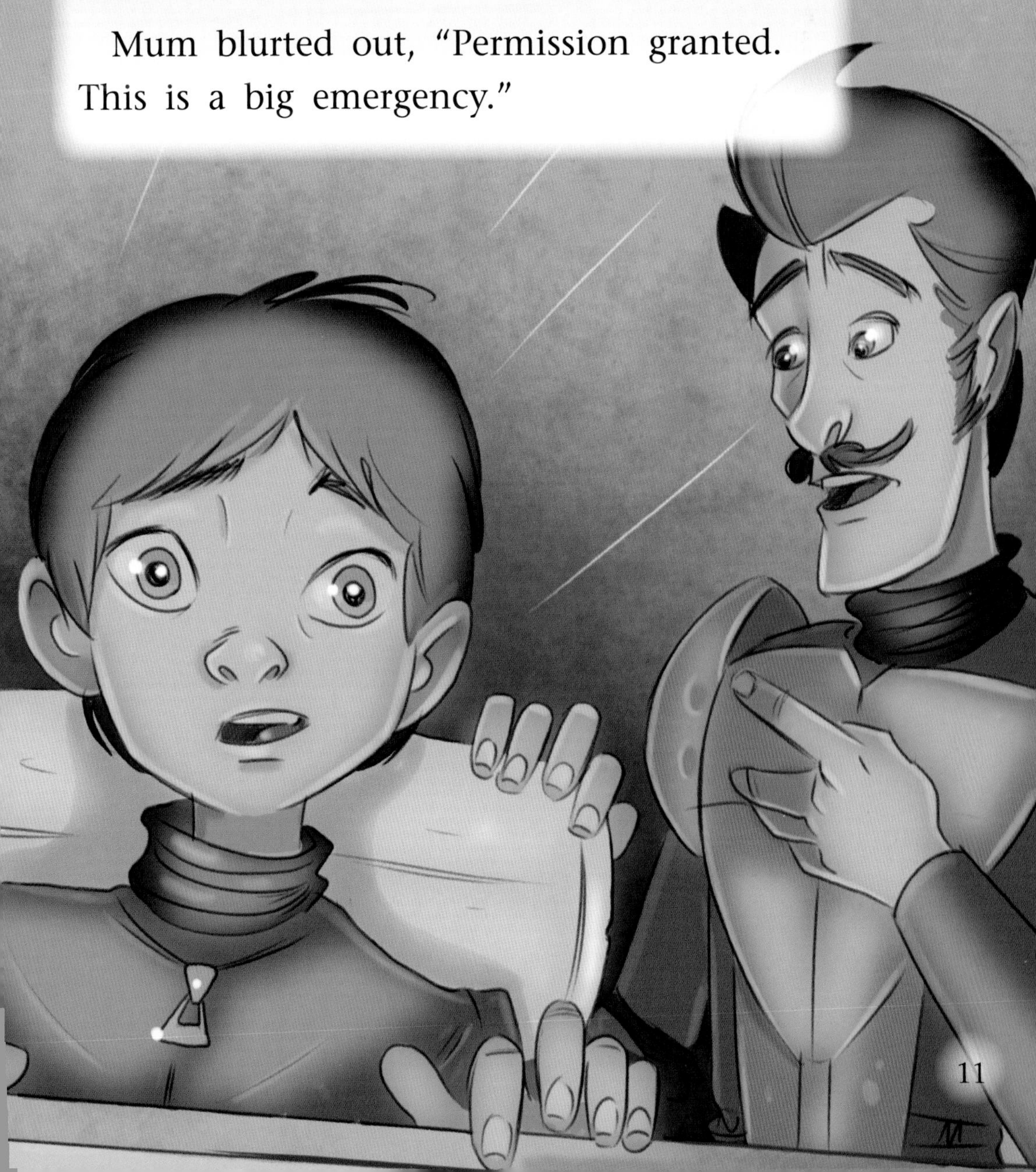

## Chapter 3

# Time for action!

"Greetings. I'm Redola," said a tall woman. She pointed to two short bearded men. "They are Betam and Epsum."

"Why are you wearing black?" asked Max. Space Guard uniforms were orange because it was an easy colour to see.

"Well, it's a nice change," said Mum. She gave Max a look that meant *don't waste time talking about clothes*.

Max kept silent.

Redola clapped her hands. "Time for action. Betam and Epsum, ready the atomic missiles."

Dad went pale. "But if the asteroid shatters, we risk a huge meteor shower over Earth!"

"It's too dangerous," said Mum. "People will get hurt."

"Meteor showers must not be allowed," said Dad.

"Change of rules," said Redola. She turned to the two men. "Get busy, my little helpers."

Betam and Epsum hurried away.

The radio buzzed again. "Earth to Space Guard 1. Our computer is jammed. We can only use our radio. We cannot launch any spaceships to assist you. You must take action yourself. Life on Earth depends on you."

Redola leaned forwards, slipped out a silver wand and whacked the radio. "Whoops! I love how my clever little wand not only jams computers but also smashes old machines."

"Who are you?" asked Mum.

There was a ripping sound.

Redola peeled off her face to show a green, toad-like head covered with huge, hairy warts. "Take a seat to watch the biggest fireworks in Earth's history."

## Chapter 4

# Split the asteroid!

Dad stood up and folded his arms. "I won't let you release those missiles. Ever!"

Redola croaked, "Just try to stop me."

Betam and Epsum hopped back into the room. Their masks were gone, too.

"We have no weapons, so we need yours," said Redola. Her green cheeks puffed up as she smiled.

Max said, "You planted booster rockets on the asteroid to change its path towards Earth."

"Bravo!" said Redola. "And the weapons will split open the asteroid, leaving valuable metals all over Earth. We will sell them to the entire universe."

"You can't destroy all of Earth's life forms!" said Mum.

"But I can, and I will!" she croaked. "You can wait in the kitchen." Redola grabbed Mum's arm and pulled her.

"What if we refuse?" asked Dad.

Redola croaked and croaked. "You're a funny man. Get in that kitchen before we cook you."

Betam pointed towards the kitchen. "You heard Redola."

Mum broke free from Redola's grip. "No!"

Epsum instead pushed Max towards the kitchen.

"Get away, Mum!" shouted Max.

But Mum walked between Dad and Max into the kitchen.

The door slammed shut.

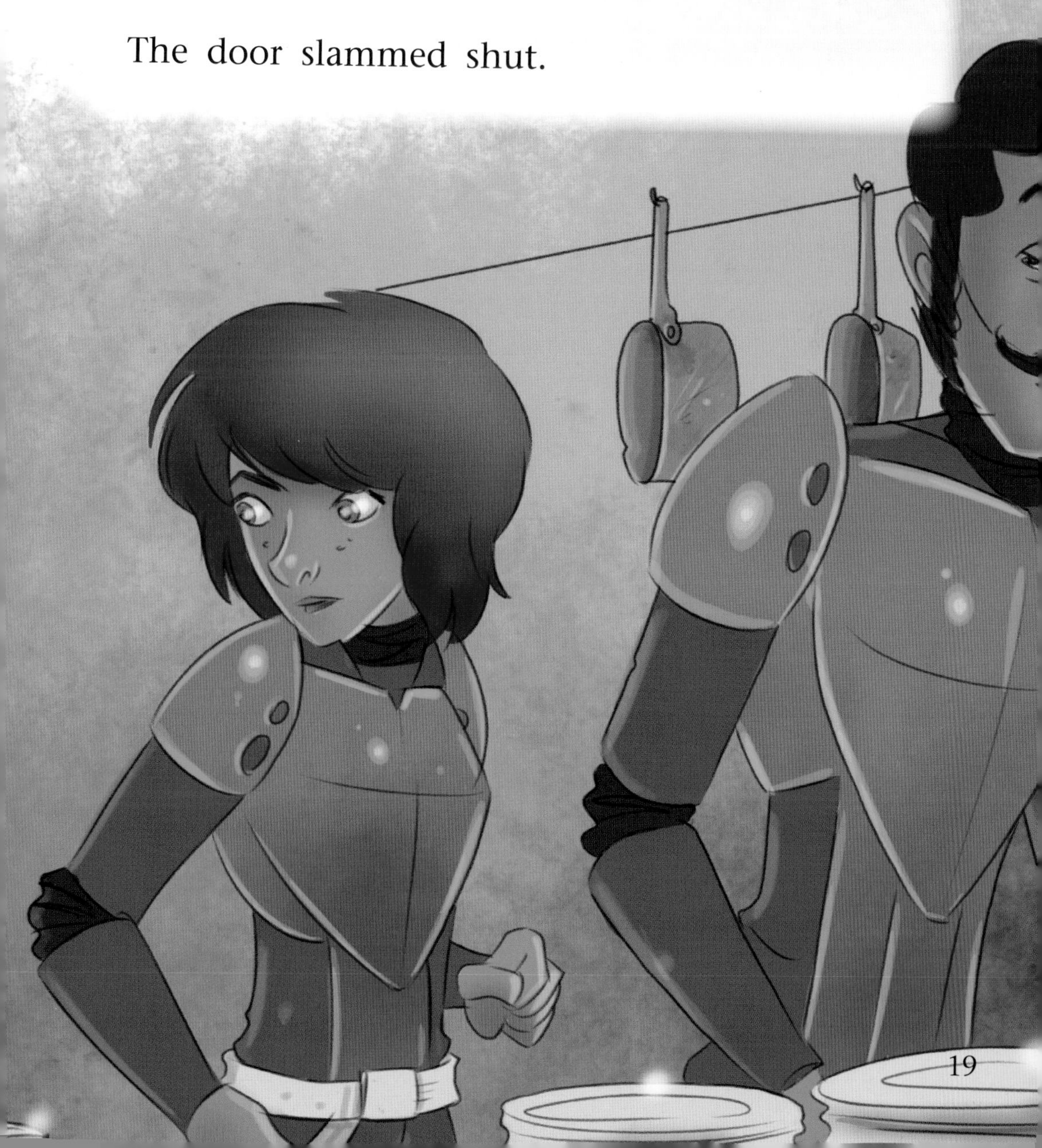

## Chapter 5

# Save the world!

"We're trapped," said Dad.

Mum banged against the door. Nothing.

Max looked around the kitchen. A white bench. Floor to ceiling cupboards. A spotlight next to a fan.

The fan.

"Hey," said Max. "I can crawl along the fan shaft into the control room."

"Great idea," said Dad. "But I'll do it."

"You won't fit," said Max. "I can help. I have a plan!"

Mum and Dad glanced at each other.

"It's our only chance," said Mum. "Max, I'm so proud of you."

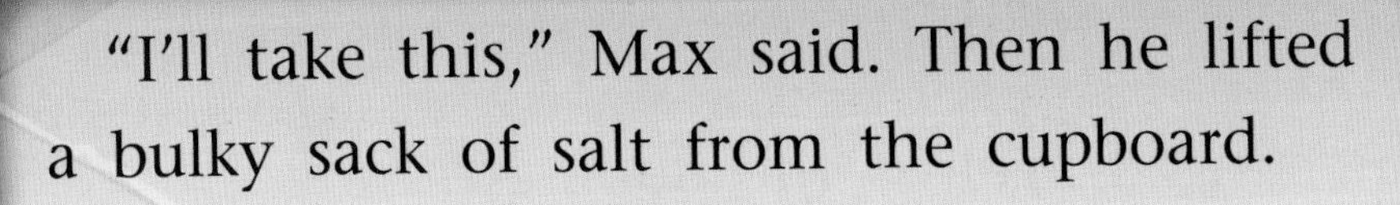

"I'll take this," Max said. Then he lifted a bulky sack of salt from the cupboard.

"Lift me up, Dad!"

Seconds later, Max wormed his way along the fan shaft.

He had to save the world.

## Chapter 6

# A salty plan

Max peered through the whirring fan blades into the control room. Redola stood below.

Max went over his plan one last time. What didn't toads like? Salt. Toads take in moisture through their skin. If they take in salt, they quickly dry out and risk death. It was time to test how much these aliens were like toads.

Max tossed handfuls of salt into the moving fan.

"Agghhh!" screamed Redola. "My skin, my beautiful skin."

Bulls-eye, or rather, toads-eye!

Betam and Epsum squealed.

Max's plan had worked! The fan was spraying salt around the room.

Max pushed out the fan and jumped onto the deck. He flung more salt at the aliens.

Redola screamed, "Ow! I need water. Quickly, back to our spaceship!"

Redola raced off, followed by Betam and Epsum.

When the three boarded their spaceship, Max pressed the eject button.

Now, he could free his parents...

Flashing red lights lit up the control room.

A metallic voice could be heard, *"The asteroid will enter Earth's atmosphere in one minute."*

Max had to hurry. That meant the asteroid was already near the air around the planet!

## Chapter 7

# Max takes control

The asteroid must be stopped. But how?

Max had an idea. He could use the spaceship as a gravity tractor. To do this, he needed to fly close enough to the asteroid, so it would feel the pull of gravity from the spaceship. The asteroid would then move towards the spaceship and be tugged away into a new orbit.

Max leaped into the pilot's seat and steered the spaceship towards the asteroid. He pulled out of the dive and looked at the words on the screen.

**NO GRAVITY PULL FOUND.**

He needed to fly closer. Max thrust the spaceship downwards.

The spaceship sped towards the asteroid. The rocky, grey surface rushed up towards Max on the screen. If he waited another second, he could crash. He quickly steered the spaceship back into space.

**NO GRAVITY PULL FOUND.**

Max gritted his teeth. He had one more chance.

The spaceship zoomed downwards.

Max heard the metallic voice of the spaceship's computer. *"Warning. Collision likely. Turn now."*

Max ignored the warning. The spaceship nearly hit the asteroid.

**GRAVITY PULL FOUND.**

Max pulled the spaceship upwards, flying it away from Earth. The asteroid followed it, like a steel pin leaps to a magnet.

His parents fell into the control room. Pieces of rubbish and food covered them from head to toe. "Max! You're OK!" said Mum.

Dad looked through the porthole. "And so is Earth! You did it, Max!"

"And you slid down the rubbish tube?" guessed Max.

Dad nodded. "Amazing! Are you pulling the asteroid away from Earth into a safe orbit?"

"Yes," Max stood up.

"Stay there," said Dad. "You can fly while you tell us exactly what happened."

"You've earned the pilot's chair. You saved Earth!" said Mum. She opened a drawer and pulled out a Space Guard uniform. "Put this on, Space Guard Max Jupiter Astro Marriot," she said.

"You're amazing!"